This is my book.

My name is:

_____

"Shoo! Shoo!
Mr. Mosquito stay out of my pants,"
Veronica yelled at the pests
buzzing around her bonnet and her butt.

A **3** little words book

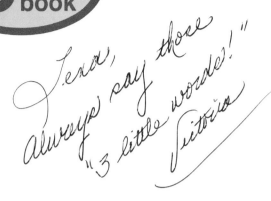
Texx,
always say those
"3 little words!"
Victoria

Mr. Mosquito
Stay Out Of My Pants

Written by
Victoria NaBozny Mayhugh

Illustrated by
Joshua Allen

ISBN: 978-1-4834-5373-6 (sc)
ISBN: 978-1-4834-5372-9 (e)

Lulu Publishing Services rev. date: 06/06/2017

In loving memory of my husband,
Wallace "Wally" Mayhugh

&

my wonderful parents,
Albert & Stella NaBozny

&

my favorite aunt,
Cioci Sophia Kaatz

Thank you for your love and the memories.

Special thank you to my editorial consultants,
Mary Ellen Brigman
Scott Albert MacKenzie
Basia Zakrzewski

It was the perfect day. Perfect except for that darn Mr. Mosquito.
The day had started with a phone call.
Sweet little Veronica came running with her sweet little Rennie in tow.

"Mommy! Mommy! Is it for me?" Veronica yelled, as she raced through the house and blew kisses to her funny frog dolls. She hoped it was cioci (aunt in Polish) on the phone. Veronica thought, "Maybe I will be going gardening, shopping in downtown Detroit or to the horse races."

"Can you be ready in 10 minutes to go gardening?" Stella, Veronica's mother, asked.
"Rennie and I are ready now," the sweet little girl shouted.

The two sisters chatted in Polish, as Veronica sat cross-legged anxiously waiting for the chatter to stop. Rennie was by her side wagging her short little tail in anticipation of their outing.
"I'll say goodbye Sophie, because our little sweetheart wants you to pick her up now," Stella said.

The sweet little girl and her sweet little dog assumed sentry duty,
as they watched for the big baby blue Cadillac to arrive.
"Mommy! Mommy! Cioci is here," Veronica yelled as Rennie barked in excitement.
Mr. Mosquito and his buddies lurked outside the window.
They were happy because Veronica was going gardening.

Veronica exchanged hugs, kisses and those "three little words" with her mother. Quickly she climbed into her palatial seat for the short ride down the lane to cioci's. Rennie assumed her back seat position ready to sniff the wind.

"Let's fly, boys. We're going gardening with Veronica," Mr. Mosquito happily buzzed. Veronica always felt like a princess riding in cioci's baby blue Caddy with those super big fins, red rocket taillights, electric windows and locks and air conditioning.

"Veronica, ready to work? I have a trunk load of flowers to plant,"
Cioci Sophie said glancing at the adorable little girl.
Actually, Veronica did not care if they even planted one flower.
She loved just being with cioci.

It was the perfect day. Birds were chirping. Squirrels were frolicking in the yard. Pesky Mr. Mosquito had not greeted Veronica – not yet – and a flock of Canada geese were coming in for a landing.

"Cioci, here they come. Here come the poopers," Veronica yelled pointing to the sky. This triggered an immediate reaction from cioci, who raced for the broom. The immediate reaction from Veronica was trying not to giggle.

They had a love/hate relationship.
The sweet little girl loved the geese.
Their flying gracefulness captivated her,
while their on-land waddling gave Veronica the giggles.
She even had named her flying
friends --- Charlie, Priscilla and Penelope.
Cioci hated the intruders.
The geese left their deposits, not only on her lawn,
but on the banks of her beloved flower garden.

"Charlie, Priscilla and Penelope are making a bank deposit, cioci,"
Veronica yelled. "And they make big deposits. They are big poopers."
Eyes met eyes as they burst into laughter, while Rennie raced up
and down the driveway barking. But Rennie never would harm the geese.

"Veronica, you are my little sweetheart," Cioci Sophie said
hugging the sweet little girl. "If those poopers make you happy, I'm happy."
However, grabbing her broom, she herded the geese down to the lake front.
"Charlie, Priscilla and Penelope, we have work to do so stay out of my flower garden."

"Break time," cioci said surprising the sweet little girl.

They chatted and laughed, as they strolled down the lane to have a picnic lunch under their favorite oak tree.

Pesky Mr. Mosquito and his buddies led the way.

But Veronica had a surprise for Mr. Mosquito today.

"Cioci, I'm hungry for your yummy meatball sandwiches. My tummy is making all these funny little noises," Veronica giggled rubbing her tummy.

"Shoo! Shoo! Mr. Mosquito stay out of my pants," Veronica yelled at the pests buzzing around her bonnet and her butt.

"Mr. Mosquito, you won't bite me today," Veronica said, spritzing herself with her mother's homemade concoction.

"Cioci, they love my derriere. That's a new word Mommy taught me."

Pulling down her pants, several red marks were revealed --- all bites from their last gardening outing. "They don't itch now. Mommy put some stinky cream on my derriere. Now, I'm going to have ants in my pants," she giggled, as a procession of ants feasted on her sandwich crumbs.

"They are going, going, gone," cioci said, brushing the intruders and crumbs off the blanket.

Veronica lovingly watched her favorite aunt. She wanted this moment to last forever.
It was summertime, and she was with cioci.
Yawning, the sweet little girl struggled to keep her eyes open. However,
Veronica lost the slumber battle and cuddled up with Rennie for an afternoon nap.
"Sleep, my sweet little Veronica," Cioci Sophie said, kissing her niece and
covering her with a blanket.
"Rennie, don't leave our little girl. How sweet, she sleeps with a smile
on her face."

Cioci Sophie worked until all flowers were planted. The garden was perfect.
Mr. Mosquito and his buddies still lurked nearby. They were mad. No bites today.
Meanwhile, dreamland for the sweet little girl took her to downtown
Detroit to shop with cioci.
Dreamland also took her to the horse races, where aunt and niece
scrutinized the horses.
"I want to bet on that one," the sweet little girl said pointing to a
chestnut beauty. "She's a winner."

Next stop in dreamland was cioci's tavern, where Veronica played pool and shuffleboard. If there were too many customers, they moved to the kitchen and always munched on cioci's yummy meatball sandwiches.
Mommy's stinky spray kept Veronica safe from Mr. Mosquito.

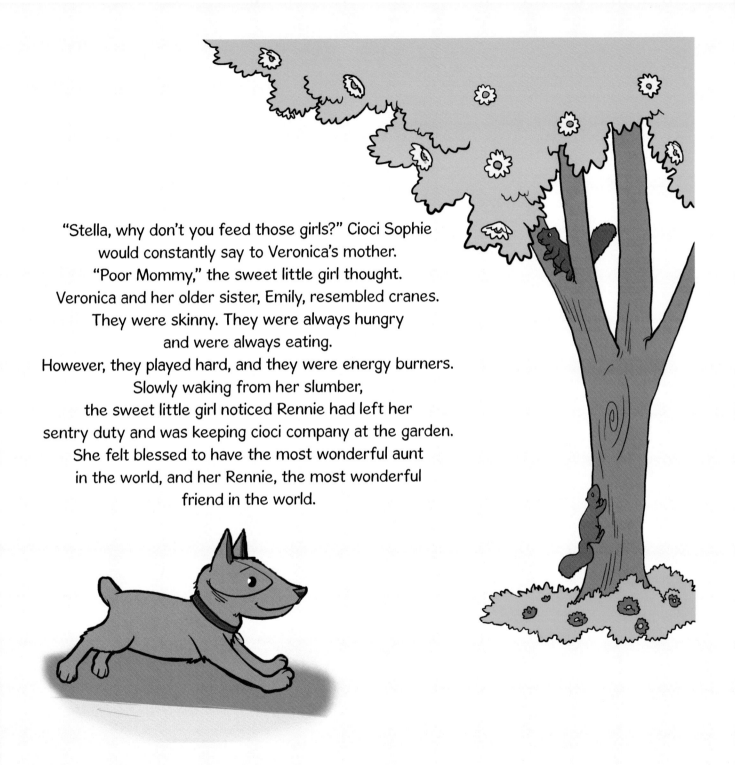

"Stella, why don't you feed those girls?" Cioci Sophie
would constantly say to Veronica's mother.
"Poor Mommy," the sweet little girl thought.
Veronica and her older sister, Emily, resembled cranes.
They were skinny. They were always hungry
and were always eating.
However, they played hard, and they were energy burners.
Slowly waking from her slumber,
the sweet little girl noticed Rennie had left her
sentry duty and was keeping cioci company at the garden.
She felt blessed to have the most wonderful aunt
in the world, and her Rennie, the most wonderful
friend in the world.

Sensing Veronica was awake, Rennie raced to her former post and smothered the sweet little girl with kisses.

"Rennie! Rennie! You are a silly little dog," Veronica said, giggling as her best friend licked her face.

Looking skyward, Veronica quickly shouted, "Cioci, here they come again. Here come the poopers --- Charlie, Priscilla and Penelope."

Gracefully they landed near the sweet little girl to feast on crumbs from the earlier picnic.

Cioci watched from a distance. She realized it was the best of times.

Suddenly, the geese started honking ready to take off in flight.
"Goodbye Charlie! Goodbye Priscilla! Goodbye Penelope!" Veronica yelled.
Rennie barked as Veronica and Cioci Sophie waved goodbye to the sweet little girl's three flying friends.
It also was time for Mr. Mosquito and his buddies to fly away.
"Goodbye Mr. Mosquito," Veronica giggled.

The three geese were joined
by other Canada geese.
"Cioci, watch my friends,"
Veronica said
hugging her aunt and Rennie.
The geese performed
an unbelievable flying show
just as the sweet little
goose whisperer predicted.
It was the perfect day.
No longer was pesky Mr. Mosquito
and his buddies buzzing around her.
She had escaped his stinger --- no new butt bites.
Veronica was happy.

"I love you, Veronica," Cioci Sophie said hugging the sweet little girl.
"I love you, cioci," Veronica said wrapped in her aunt's arms.
It was the best of times. They were blessed.
And always they said those three little words --- "I love you" --- to each other.

LOOK IT UP

Veronica always finds the meaning of a word that she does not know.
Here is her word list from Mr. Mosquito Stay Out Of My Pants.

ANTICIPATION ----- To look forward
ANXIOUSLY -------- Eager to do something
BELOVED ---------- Dearly loved
CAPTIVATING ------ To hold your attention
CIOCI ------------- Aunt in Polish
CONCOCTION ------ Mixture of something
CUDDLED ---------- To hold close for comfort
DEPOSIT ----------- To put something somewhere
DERRIERE ---------- Your butt in French
FROLICKING ------- Playful
GRACEFULNESS --- Beautiful movement
HERDED ----------- To gather
IMPATIENTLY ------ Cannot wait
INTRUDERS -------- Not invited
LURKED ----------- To be in a hidden place
MISCHIEVOUS ----- Playful desire to cause trouble
PALATIAL ---------- Royal place
RELATIONSHIP ----- Connection between two people or things
SCRUTINIZED ------ To examine carefully
SENTRY ----------- Guard, watch
SMOTHERED ------- To cover
SPRITZING --------- Spraying
STRUGGLED ------- Great effort
TAVERN ----------- Place where spirits/food is served.
WADDLING -------- To move clumsily

I love learning a new word. Learn a new word with me.

COLOR IT

Veronica loves to color.

Have fun coloring Veronica and Rennie running into the house.

Veronica loves gardening with cioci.
Color Veronica and cioci unloading flowers to plant in the garden.

CIOCI

COLOR IT

Veronica has a smile on her face, while she dreams
of playing pool at cioci's tavern.

Veronica loves to draw her funny frog dolls.
Draw one of her frogs or design one of your own frog dolls.

Veronica loves to play pool at cioci's tavern.

Draw something you love to do.

Victoria NaBozny Mayhugh was a reporter/education writer
and editor at newspapers in Iowa and Ohio.
Mr. Mosquito Stay Out Of My Pants
is the first in her A "3 little words" Book series.

Four more books are awaiting publication.
Her sweet little niece and nephews, Veronica Jean,
Griffin Tiberius and Norman Joseph, respectively,
play a special part in her books.

The author hopes her books inspire her readers
of all ages
to say those "3 little words" – I Love You – to each other.
Victoria lives in West Bloomfield, MI.
Her loving husband, Wally, has been the
inspiration for her books.

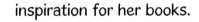